Wanda meets Berry

Down in the

Firefly Forest,

It's a very special place.

Where there's
magic
all around,

In EVERY nook,
and base
and space.

There's a fairy who's called
Wanda,

Who just loves to hide and chase.

She is known to all the fae folk,
'round the place.
For she dances

Her fairy magic

glitters everywhere,

Or so I'm told.

She likes to bring the light,
Of everything that she beholds.

Wanda's **wonder** causes *mischief,*

Just a little now and then.

For she's always on the move,
She never stops to count to ten.

1 2 3 4 5 6 7 8 9 10

Berry is a Pixie,

Part of the Firefly Keepers Tribe.

He's always in a book
or taking notes,

He loves to scribe.

He's an earnest sort of fellow,
Finding *facts* and making plans.

Writing data
looking up truths,

★ ★ ★

Measuring things out in grams.

One special thing
that he adores,

The
Aramberry Pie.

The sweet and tasty treat,

Brings out the twinkle
in his eye.

One lovely sunny
summers day,
Berry takes a longer stroll.

He decides he needs to know,

The kind musings of
Mr Mole.

He set out on his journey,

With a piece of

special pie.

In his pocket just in case,

He's feeling peckish on the fly.

As he ambles through the forest,
Unbeknownst a little further.

Is the fairy known as
Wanda,

Singing louder than a murmur.

As *Wanda* wonders further,

Getting closer unaware.

That **Berry** and his,

notes,

Are round the
corner over there.

Her singing's getting louder,

Makes poor Berry jump in

fright.

For his mind was in the distance,

Not the forest with his

sight.

Now Berry stops
then sees that,

Wanda's floating there before him.

Their eyes both look
in shock, surprised,

What fate had found
and brought them?

Here together in the hallow,
Of the forest at this time.

What would their tribes both think?
Let's hope it's surely not a crime.

'Cause Fae and
Pixies do not mix,

The fact of it is true.

They both have

different

roles to play,

This really would not do!

But something

very magical,

Began to shape,

take form.

T'was completely unforeseen,

This was really not the norm.

A smile emerged
from both of them,

They found they were

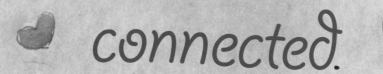 connected.

As though they'd known each other,

Since the day they manifested.

No words can

say, describe or tell,

The changes that they felt.

A shift took place,
They both were sure;
a friendship was now dealt.

They spent the
afternoon in play,

Discussing all the world.

For when they were together,

Both their magic grew and swirled.

The End

Who are your friends?

Think about who your friends are.

They could be children from school, nursery or playgroup, family members, people that you know, neighbours and your pets if you have any.

What is it about them that makes them so special to you?

Maybe you could tell them why they are so special the next time you see them.